WITH LOVE, AT CHRISTMAS

WITH LOVE, AT CHRISTMAS

Mem Fox

ILLUSTRATED BY
GARY LIPPINCOTT

Abingdon Press / Nashville

WITH LOVE, AT CHRISTMAS

Library of Congress Cataloging-in-Publication Data

Fox, Mem, 1945-
    With love, at Christmas / Mem Fox; illus-
trated by Gary Lippincott.
        p.   cm.
    Summary: After buying, wrapping, and stor-
ing in a chest the Christmas gifts for her large
family, an Italian grandmother discovers others
more in need.
        ISBN 0-687-45863-3 (alk. paper)

    [1. Christmas—Fiction. 2. Charity—Fiction.]
I. Lippincott, Gary, ill.   II. Title.
PZ7.F8373Wj 1988
[E]—dc 19   88-6332
                                                  CIP
                                                  AC

This book is printed on acid-free paper.

PRINTED IN SINGAPORE

For Kate (Boz) Juttner,
with love, any time

There was once an old Italian woman called
Mrs. Cavallaro who had lived in her neighborhood most of her
life. Her husband had died some years before. Among her friends
and relations she was well known for her kindness and
generosity, especially at Christmas.

Every year, as early as October, Mrs. Cavallaro began her shopping. In the smart shops and the craft shops, in the markets and the malls she bought presents for everyone she knew—her children and her grandchildren, her other relations and all her friends, everyone, that is, except her older grandsons to whom she gave money.

"They wouldn't be happy with socks or handkerchiefs," she thought.

By the end of November she had wrapped every present, and on each gift tag she had written, *"With love, at Christmas."*

She kept all her presents in a large wooden chest in her bedroom, and long before Christmas, her younger grandchildren would plead with her to let them look inside.

"Only a little peep, Grandma. Please!"

But her eyes just twinkled and she kept the chest firmly closed.

One year, close to Christmas, news came to Mrs. Cavallaro of a terrible famine in Africa.

"What can I do to help?" she wondered. "I have no money left. I have spent it all on Christmas presents."

Hardly realizing what she was doing, she took the money she had intended for her grandsons and mailed it away to buy food for the hungry.

A few mornings later in the newspaper, she read about a family of nine, so poor that they could not afford presents for Christmas.

Hardly realizing what she was doing, she packed up the toys she had intended for her younger grandchildren and sent them to the family who would otherwise have had none.

Just before Christmas, the husband of one of her neighbors
was hurt in an accident at work.

"He may never work again," cried the neighbor. "How shall we
live?"

Hardly realizing what she was doing, Mrs. Cavallaro gathered
the gifts of clothing and linen intended for her children,
took them to the neighbor's house, and left them on the porch.

And so it happened that on Christmas Eve the wooden chest was empty. When she realized what she had done, Mrs. Cavallaro broke down and wept.

"What shall I do? Now I have nothing left to give to my family. The chest is empty and so is my purse."

When she went to bed that night she tossed and turned for a long time before she fell asleep.

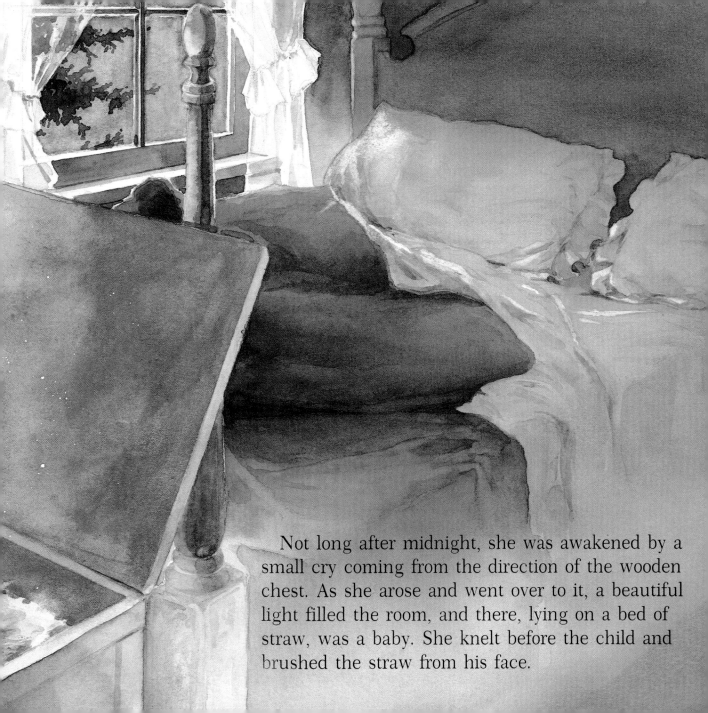

Not long after midnight, she was awakened by a small cry coming from the direction of the wooden chest. As she arose and went over to it, a beautiful light filled the room, and there, lying on a bed of straw, was a baby. She knelt before the child and brushed the straw from his face.

On Christmas morning, Mrs. Cavallaro was found dead, kneeling at her wooden chest. The baby was nowhere to be seen.

"Oh, no!" cried her family. "She was taking out our presents to put them under the tree."

For it is true that the chest which had been empty was once again filled with gifts, and on each one was written . . .

"With love, at Christmas."